This book belongs to

For Mum
—J.E.

For Heidi, Chloe & Ben
My Own Loving Family Forever
—D.H.

Text copyright © 2007 by Jonathan Emmett.
Illustrations copyright © 2007 by Daniel Howarth.

All rights reserved. Published by Scholastic Inc.
SCHOLASTIC, CARTWHEEL BOOKS, and associated logos are trademarks and/or registered trademarks of Scholastic Inc.

Library of Congress Cataloging-in-Publication Data
Emmett, Jonathan.
I love you always and forever / by Jonathan Emmett ;
illustrated by Daniel Howarth. p. cm.
Summary: Longtail tells Littletail that no matter what else changes
one thing will always stay the same throughout their lives.
ISBN 0-439-91654-2 (hardcover)   ISBN 0-439-88049-1 (school market)
[1. Love--Fiction. 2. Parent and child--Fiction. 3. Animals--Fiction.]
I. Howarth, Daniel, ill. II. Title.
PZ7.E696Lo 2007
[E]--dc22   2006010323

ISBN-13: 978-0-439-91654-7
ISBN-10: 0-439-91654-2

10 9 8 7 6 5 4 3 2 1   7 8 9 10 11/0

Printed in China
First Scholastic printing, January 2007

I LOVE YOU
ALWAYS AND FOREVER

By Jonathan Emmett • Illustrated by Daniel Howarth

Cartwheel
·B·O·O·K·S·®

Scholastic Inc.

New York   Toronto London Auckland Sydney
Mexico City   New Delhi   Hong Kong   Buenos Aires

Longtail and Littletail were playing in the forest.
They scampered through the bushes
and scurried round the trees.

Littletail wanted to play a game.
"Catch me if you can!" she laughed.
And she leapt into the long grass.

Littletail was fast –
but Longtail was faster.
And he caught her and swept her into his arms.

"You always catch me!"
gasped Littletail.
"Do I always?" said Longtail.
"Well, it won't be forever.
One day you will be too fast
for me to catch!"

Littletail wanted to play another game.
"Hide-and-seek!" she said.
And she bounded off into the bushes.

Longtail counted to a hundred and then went to look.

Littletail was clever –
but Longtail was cleverer.

And he found her and caught her by surprise.

"You always find me,"
giggled Littletail.
"Do I always?" said Longtail.
"Well, it won't be forever.
One day you will be too clever
for me to find!"

It was getting late, but
Littletail wanted to play one last game.
"Follow the leader!" she said.

And she wriggled down between
the roots of an old tree. Longtail took
a deep breath and followed her.

Longtail was small –
but Littletail was smaller.

And she could squeeze through
where Longtail could not.

"I always get through,"
said Littletail proudly.
"Do you always?" laughed
Longtail. "Well, it won't be
forever. One day you will be
just as big as me!"

Littletail was tired now.
So Longtail carried her home and
laid her down gently in a corner
of their nest.

"I love you, Littletail,"
said Longtail, as he kissed her good night.
"You always say that," murmured Littletail sleepily.
"Do I always?" said Longtail, as he lay down
beside her. "Well, that will be forever."

"I love you always and forever," he whispered with a smile.